My Adventure
Coloring Book

PaRragon

Bath · New York · Cologne · Melbourne · Delhi
Hong Kong · Shenzhen · Singapore

Time for a space adventure!

Want to fly to another planet?

What color is this fuzzy monster's fur?

The king and his court live in a castle.

This dragon wants a new friend.

Where will the pilot go today?

The alien ship zips through space.

Construction zone! Here comes a bulldozer!

Can you draw a web for the spider?

This robot is programed to dance!

The knight is ready to protect the kingdom!

Monster truck time!

On a quest for hidden treasure.

Give this silly monster a silly shirt.

The pterodactyl soars at night.

This robot loves to smile!

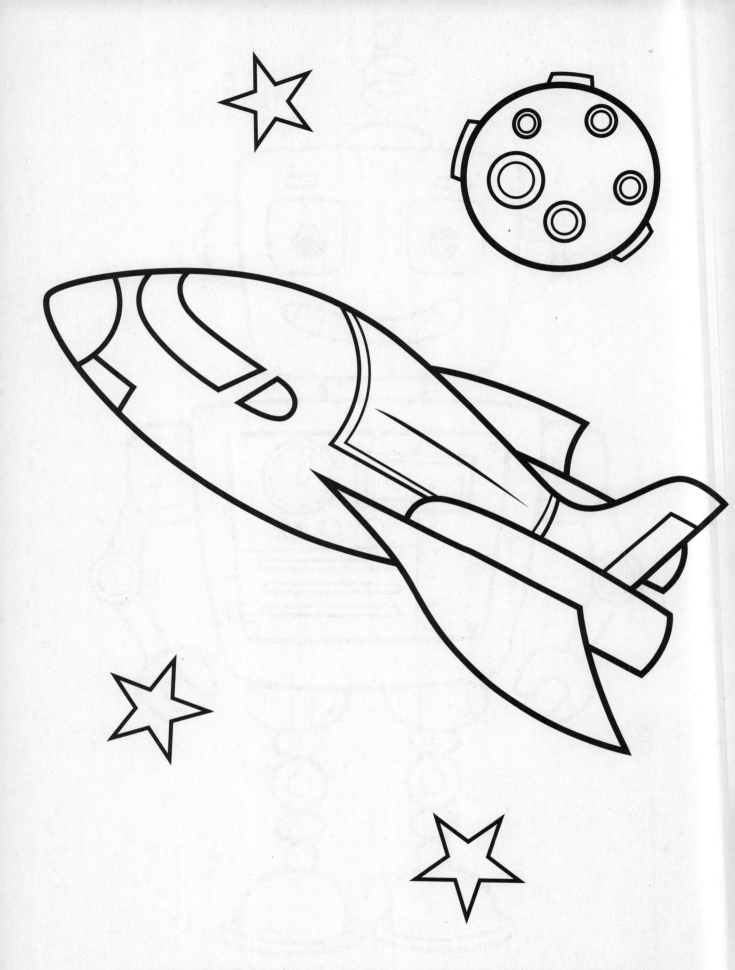

A rocket zooms through outer space!

A Martian has landed!

Arrr! Let's find some treasure, matey!

Smile, T-rex!

Want to explore the bottom of the sea?

The prince awaits his next adventure.

Uh-oh! There's a dragon on the castle.

The knight is ready for battle.

Ready for an underwater adventure?

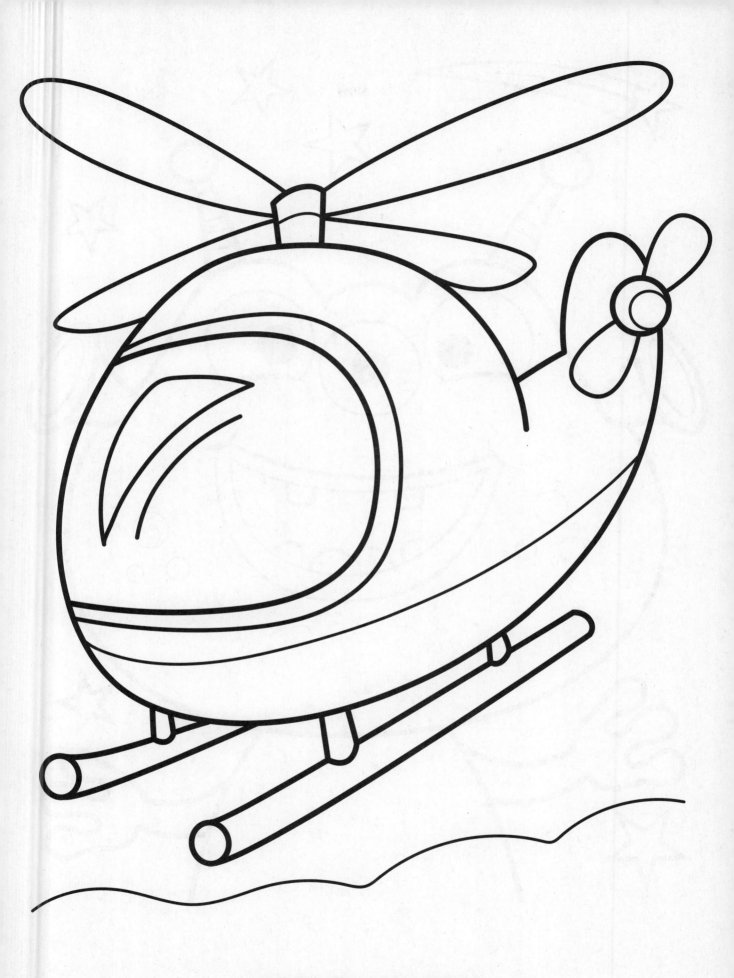

Helicopter ride!

Take me to your leader!

Look out! This dragon is hot stuff!

These robots are best friends.

Can you do the secret robot greeting?

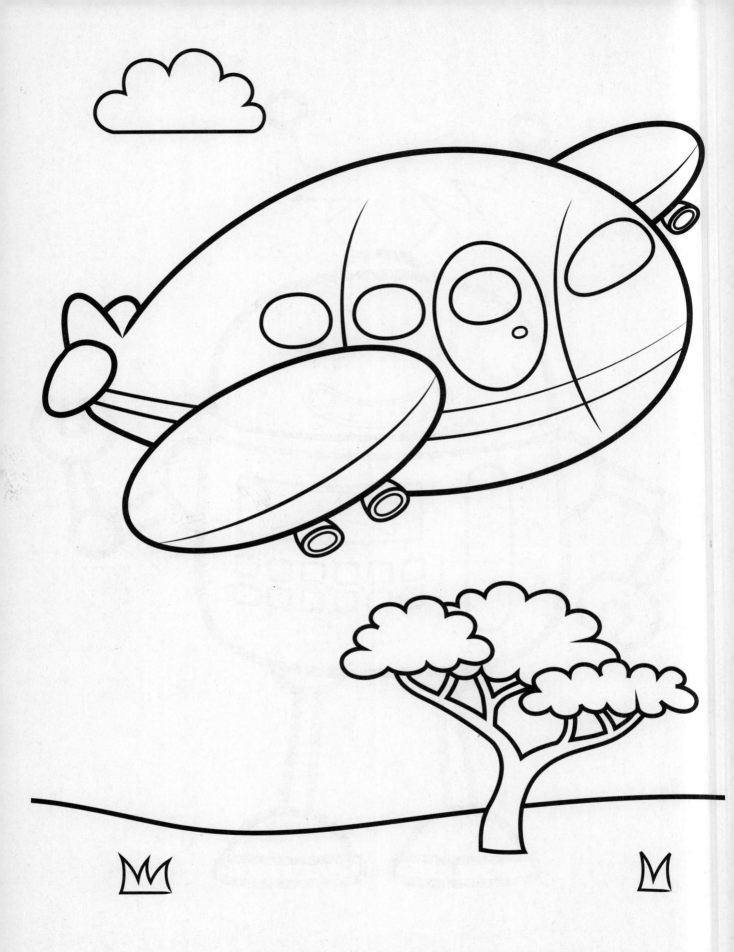

Zoom! Who is coming to visit?

The dragon flies high above the mountains.

The pirate found some coconuts.

Vroom! Vroom! Let's ride!

A race car driver always wears a helmet.

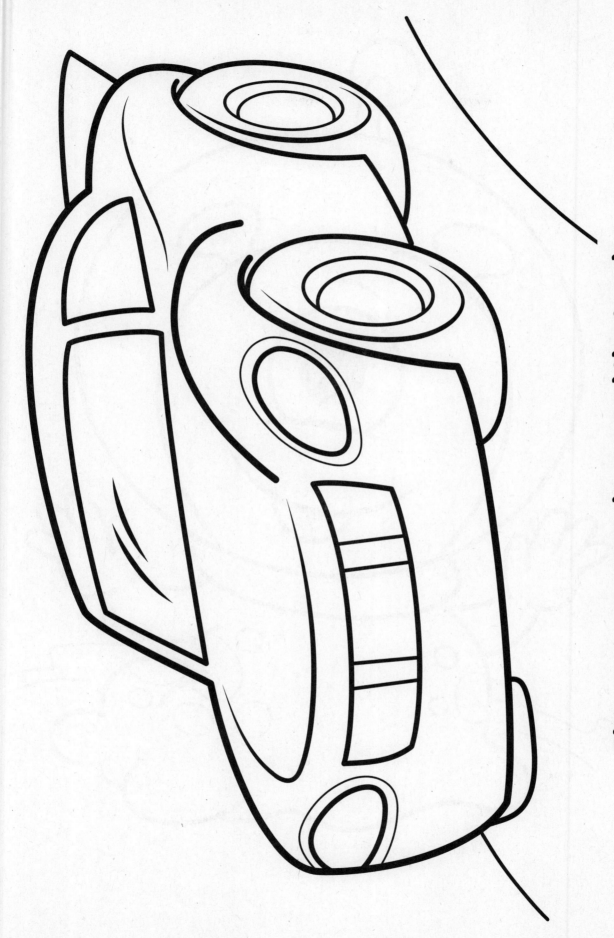

The race car speeds around the track.

This wiggly alien has an eye for adventure!

Let's pretend to be Robin Hood!

Samurai warrior!

Look! A dinosaur egg is hatching!

Next stop? Home!

Robot alert! Robot alert!

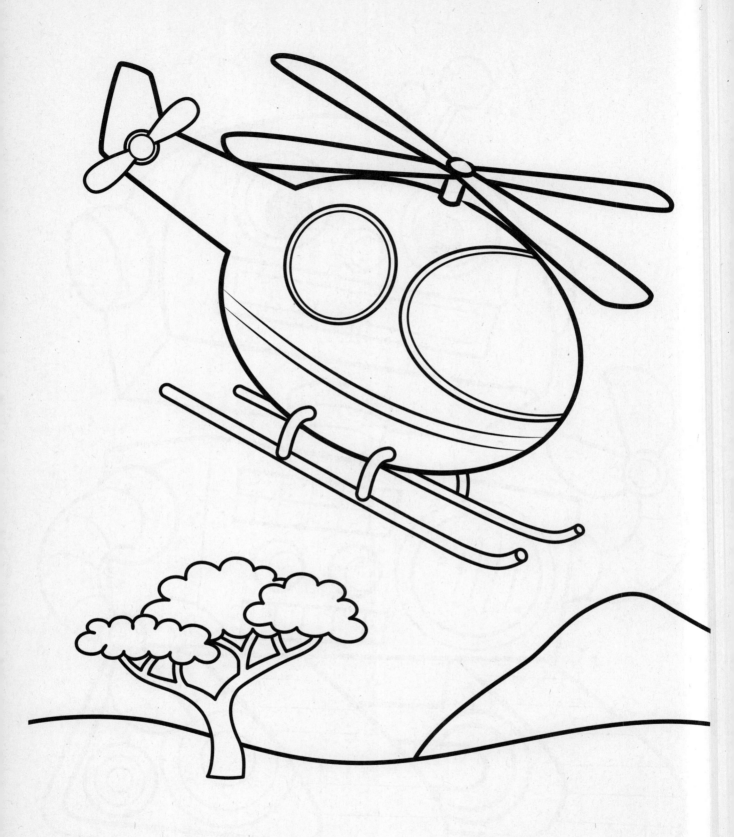

The helicopter finds a place to land!

Draw some apples for the giant to pick.

Sailing the seven seas.

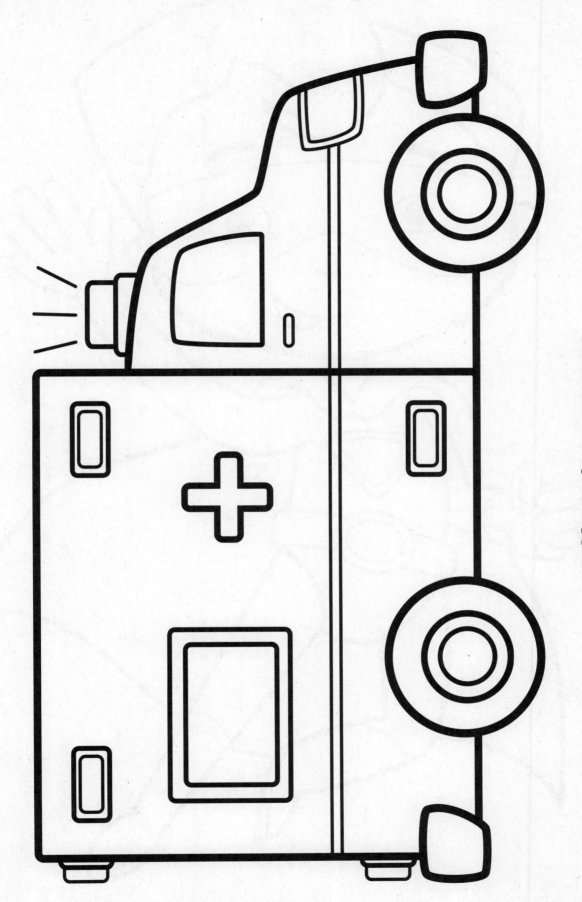

Off to the rescue!

The superhero saves the day!